D1165368

Listen! Listen!

Published by
Princeton Architectural Press
A McEvoy Group company
37 East Seventh Street
New York, New York 10003
www.papress.com

This book was hand illustrated by Paul Rand to represent
an expressive modernist approach to image making.
His technique combines collage, paper cutting, and brush-
and-ink scrawls to create a childlike visual language.

Editor: Rob Shaeffer

Special thanks to: Nicola Brower, Janet Behning,
Erin Cain, Tom Cho, Benjamin English, Jenny Florence,
Jan Cigliano Hartman, Lia Hunt, Mia Johnson,
Valerie Kamen, Simone Kaplan-Senchak, Stephanie Leke,
Diane Levinson, Jennifer Lippert, Sara McKay,
Jaime Nelson Noven, Sara Stemen, Paul Wagner,
Joseph Weston, and Janet Wong of Princeton
Architectural Press —Kevin C. Lippert, publisher

Library of Congress Cataloging-in-Publication Data:
Names: Rand, Ann, 1918 or 1919-2012, author. | Rand, Paul,
1914-1996, illustrator.
Title: Listen! listen! / by Ann Rand ; illustrated by Paul Rand.
Description: First Princeton Architectural Press edition. |
New York : Princeton Architectural Press, 2016. | Summary:
Rhyming text reveals the many sounds that can be heard if one
listens closely.
Identifiers: LCCN 2015042814 | ISBN 9781616894948
(hardback)
Subjects: | CYAC: Stories in rhyme. | Sound--Fiction. |
Listening--Fiction. | BISAC: JUVENILE FICTION / Concepts
/ Sounds.
Classification: LCC PZ8.3.R15 Li 2016 | DDC [E]--dc23
LC record available at http://lccn.loc.gov/2015042814

For Cath

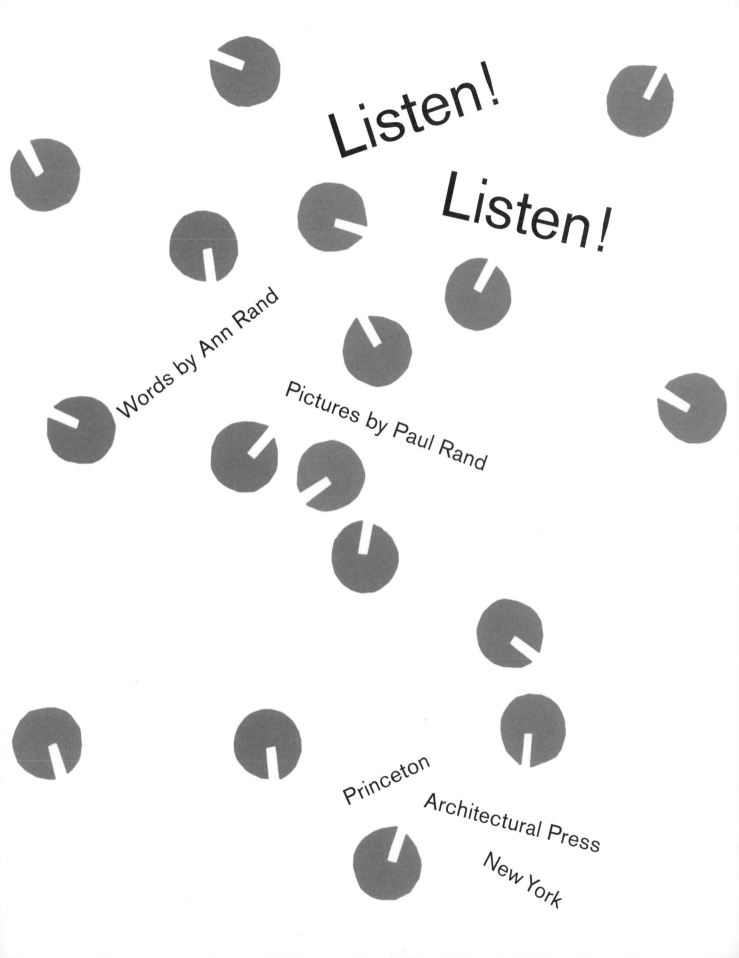

Listen! Listen!

Words by Ann Rand

Pictures by Paul Rand

Princeton Architectural Press

New York

Listen…

I can hear
a very tiny plop.
It might be a
raindrop.

4

Now there's a much bigger whop,
for I hit the fence
with my ball.

7

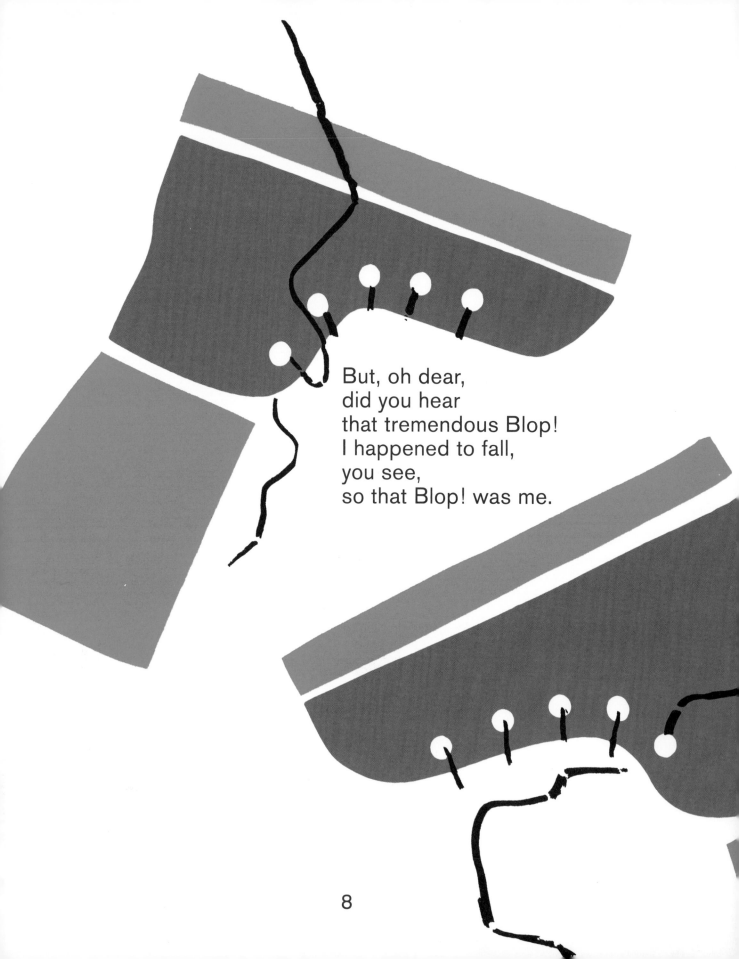

But, oh dear,
did you hear
that tremendous Blop!
I happened to fall,
you see,
so that Blop! was me.

Listen...
It's very clear.
There is something
without any sound
that I hear.
Can you guess?
Do you know
that it's snow?

10

Rrrroooaaarrrrr!

Now that's not a door,
because a door goes wham!
if you slam it,
nor a dog,
and as for a cat,
it certainly isn't that.
A bear would growl
and a wolf would howl.
None of you knows
what that roar was.

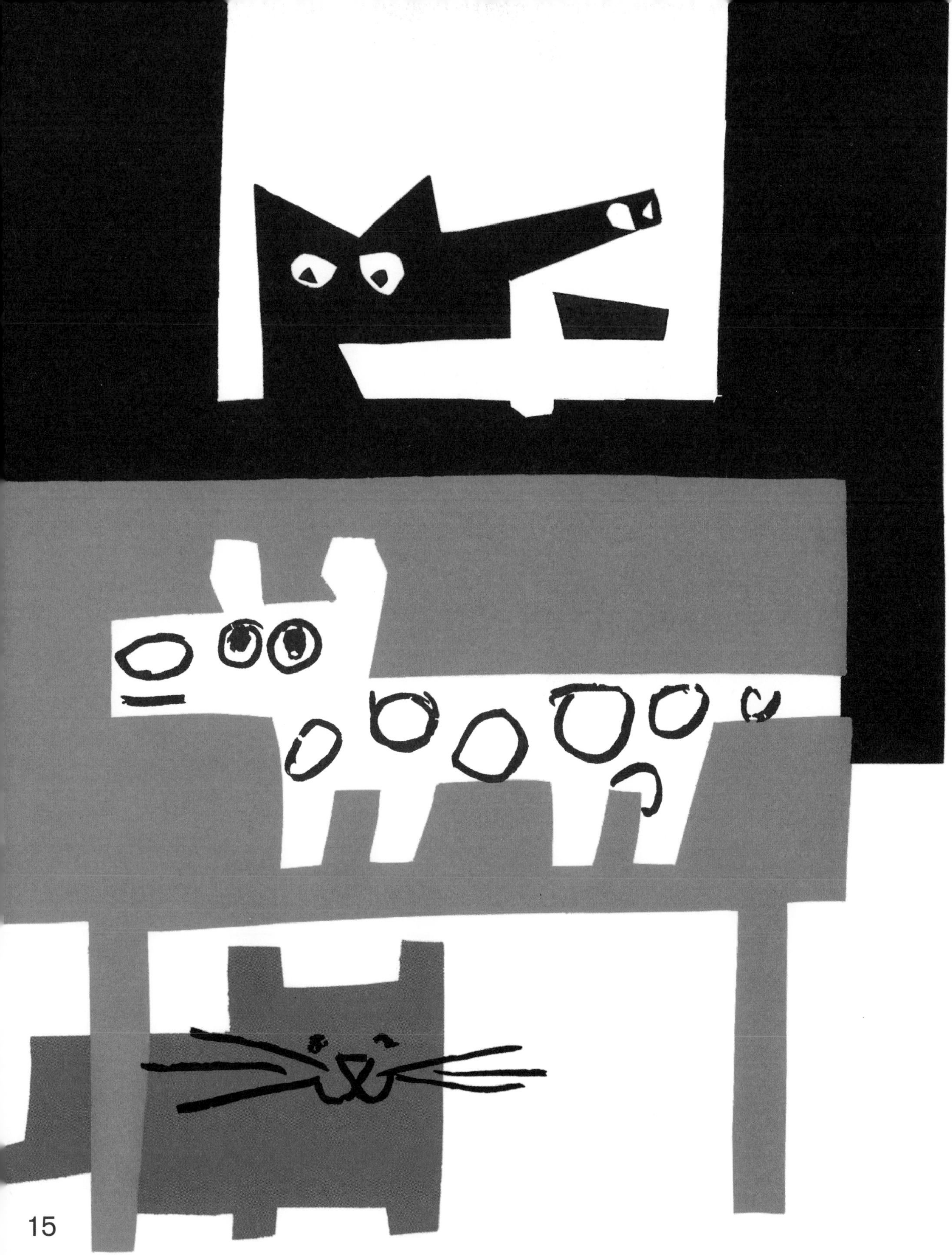

I'm the only one who does,
because that roar
was mine
when I pretended to be
a lion.

16

Listen...
If I make a noise
like clink clank,
it means I'm putting pennies
in my bank.

18

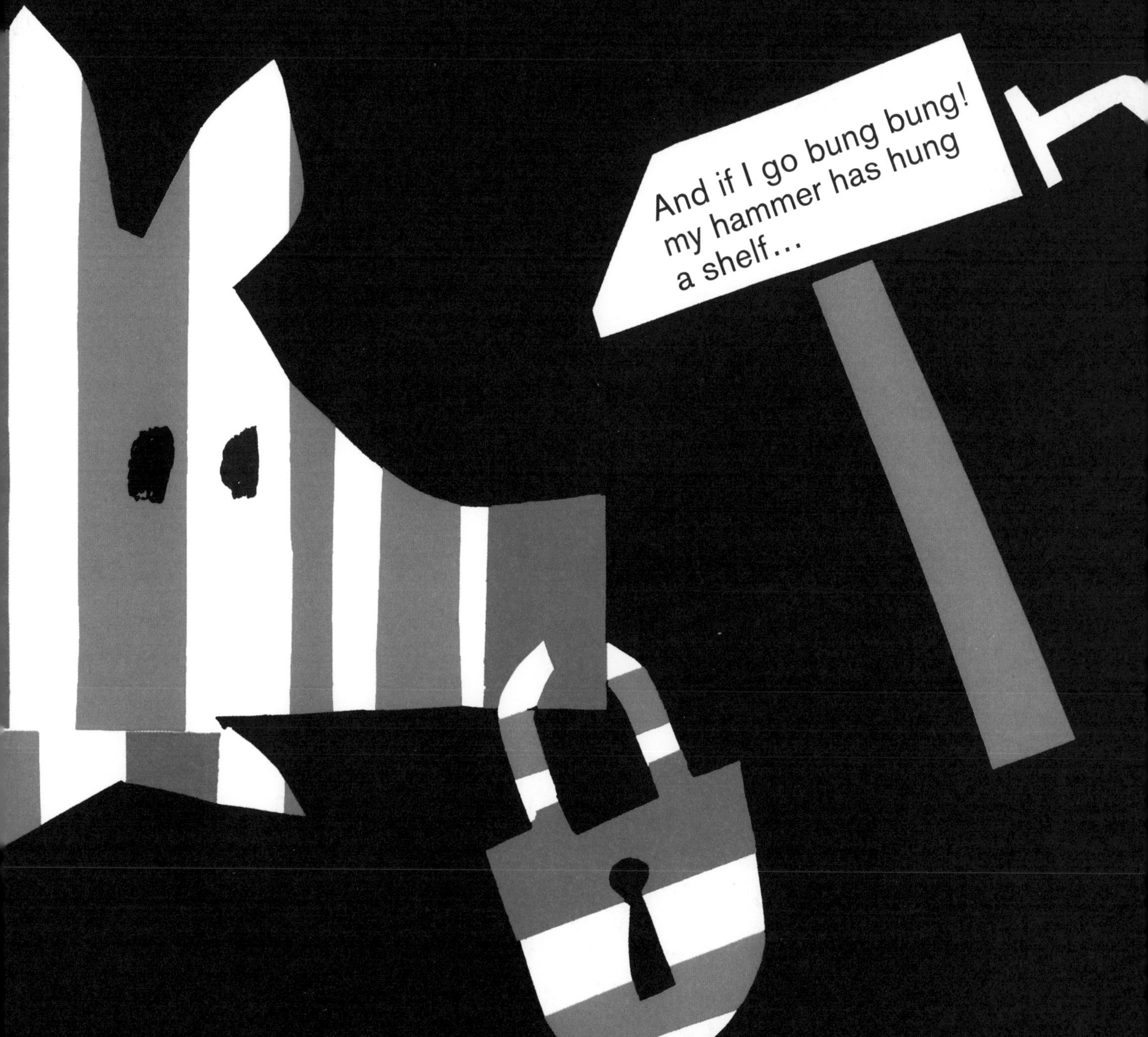
And if I go bung bung!
my hammer has hung
a shelf…

or built a box
in case I catch
a fox.

Shhhhhhh…
If you're very quiet
and there's a little
breeze,
you can hear the whisper
of the trees.

22

(But when a big wind comes,
those same trees
moan and groan
and I run home.)

23

Listen…

It's not too polite a thing,
but if you'll bring
your ear up close,
you can hear the breakfast noise
I like the most.
It's the crunch crunch
of buttered toast.

Some sounds are scary
and some are nice.
I like the scritchity-scratch
of mice,
but my mother
takes a broom and very soon
Whoom!
that mouse
is out of the house.

I like the whir
that the wings
of a hummingbird make
when it flies,

and the Psssssst!
of fireworks as they
sputter in the sky.

27

But what a fright
I get in bed at night
when a siren goes
Eeeeeee!
if I don't pull the covers
right over my head.

But the noise I like
the very best
is early morning before sunrise
because then
(when I keep my eyes tight shut)
I can hear
the world wake up.
It's a wonderful mixed-up sound.
From far and near
from air and ground,
it comes from all around.
Listen…

Listen…